PJ MASKS
Time to Be a Hero

Based on the screenplay
"Blame It on the Train, Owlette"

Ready-to-Read

Simon Spotlight
New York   London   Toronto   Sydney   New Delhi

SIMON SPOTLIGHT
An imprint of Simon & Schuster Children's Publishing Division
1230 Avenue of the Americas, New York, New York 10020
This Simon Spotlight edition October 2018
Adapted by Daphne Pendergrass from the series PJ Masks
All rights reserved, including the right of reproduction in whole or in part in any form.
SIMON SPOTLIGHT, READY-TO-READ, and colophon are registered trademarks of
Simon & Schuster, Inc.
For information about special discounts for bulk purchases, please contact
Simon & Schuster Special Sales at 1-866-506-1949 or business@simonandschuster.com.
Manufactured in China 0718 SDI

Connor, Amaya, and Greg
are at the fair.
"I want to ride the train!"
Amaya says.
But where is it?

The train is gone!

The PJ Masks can find it!

Greg becomes Gekko!

Connor becomes Catboy!

Amaya becomes Owlette!

They are the PJ Masks!

Owlette really wants
to ride the train.

She is in a rush
to find it.

Owlette jumps into
the Cat-Car.
"Come on!" she says.

She uses her Owl Eyes
to see far away.

Owlette sees the train!

Romeo is driving it!

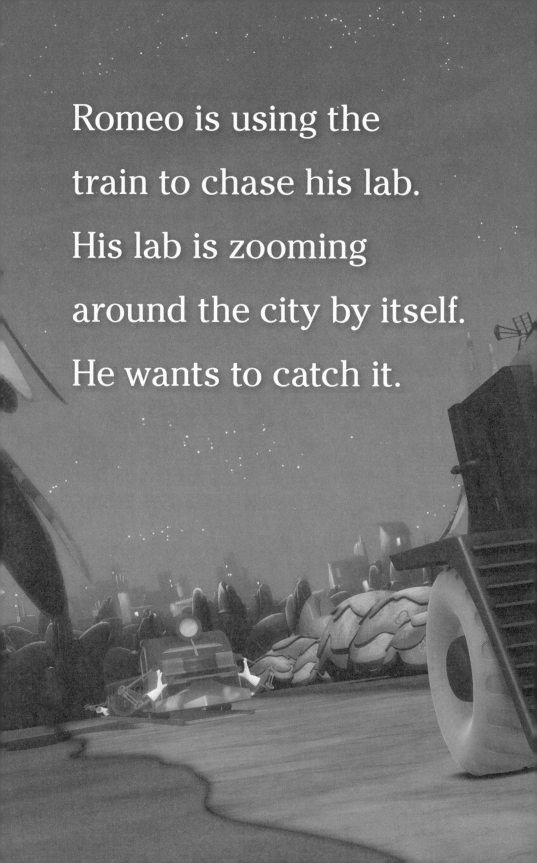

Romeo is using the train to chase his lab. His lab is zooming around the city by itself. He wants to catch it.

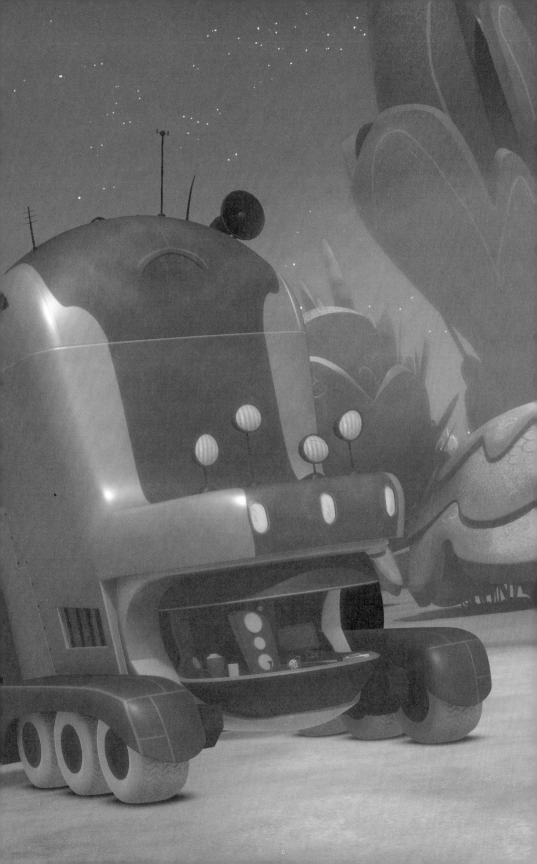

The PJ Masks jump

onto the train!

Owlette rushes ahead
to stop Romeo.

"Wait for us!" Gekko
and Catboy say.
Romeo catches Owlette!

Gekko and Catboy

help her escape.

"I am sorry," Owlette says. "I should have listened and not rushed. It is time to be a hero!"

Owlette has a plan.

The PJ Masks will

work together.

Catboy gathers
some branches.

He throws them to Owlette.

Gekko climbs onto the train.

Owlette throws the
branches to Gekko.
He jams the train tracks
with them!

The train is out of control.

Gekko is very strong.

He stops the train.

The train cars swing around the lab and trap it.

Romeo leaves the train.
He is so happy to have
his lab back.

PJ Masks all shout hooray!

Because in the night,

we saved the day!

The PJ Masks return
the train to the fair.
The day is saved!

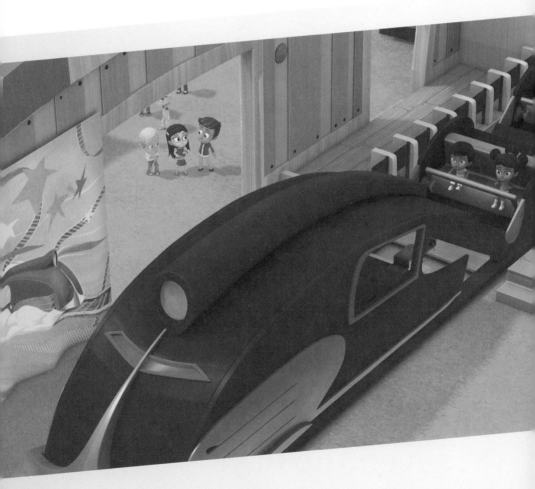

Hero School

Based on the episode
"Looking After Gekko"

Ready-to-Read

Simon Spotlight
New York   London   Toronto   Sydney   New Delhi

SIMON SPOTLIGHT
An imprint of Simon & Schuster Children's Publishing Division
1230 Avenue of the Americas, New York, New York 10020
This Simon Spotlight edition October 2018
Adapted by Tina Gallo from the series PJ Masks
All rights reserved, including the right of reproduction in whole or in part in any form.
SIMON SPOTLIGHT, READY-TO-READ, and colophon are registered trademarks of
Simon & Schuster, Inc.
For information about special discounts for bulk purchases, please contact
Simon & Schuster Special Sales at 1-866-506-1949 or business@simonandschuster.com.
Manufactured in China 0718 SDI

Greg is excited to take a book home from school.

Greg reaches for a book.

It is too high.

Greg falls.

Connor and Amaya get
the book for Greg.
They walk to the
school bus.

Oh no! The school bus
is missing!
This looks like a job for
the PJ Masks!

Amaya becomes

Owlette!

Greg becomes
Gekko!

Connor becomes
Catboy!

They are the PJ Masks!

Gekko wants to drive.

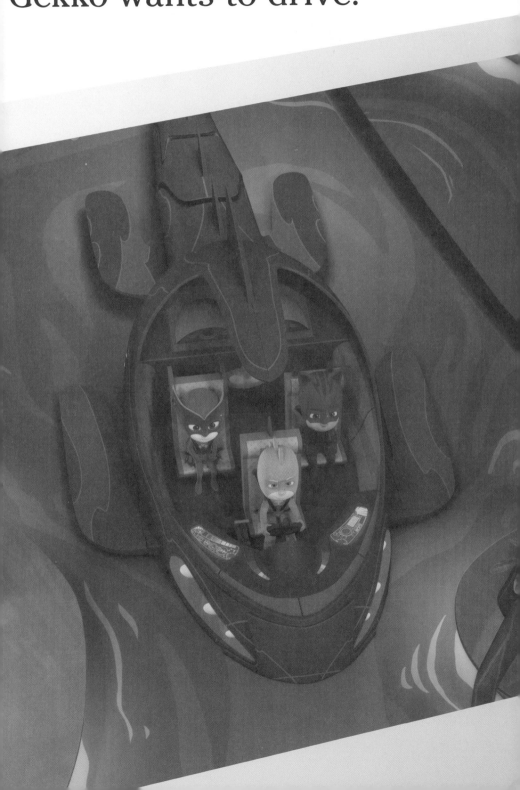

The PJ Masks see the
school bus! They chase it.

The Gekko-Mobile
is too slow.

The bus gets away.

"Cat Ears!" says Catboy.

"Owl Eyes!" says Owlette.

They find the bus

using their powers.

The bus is in the town square! Gekko wants to be the hero.

Gekko drives to
the town square.
Night Ninja has the bus!

The Ninjalinos are
painting the bus blue.
"Give back the bus,"
Gekko says.

"No! The bus will be
my super-car!"
Night Ninja says.

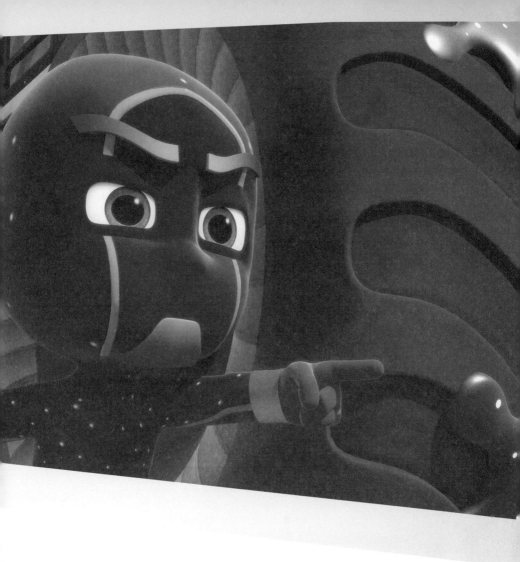

Night Ninja throws

Sticky-Splats.

Gekko is in trouble!

Owlette and Catboy arrive.

"We will help, Gekko!"

they say.

Gekko does not want help.

Night Ninja throws
Sticky-Splats at Catboy.

Owlette gets tangled.

"Only I can stop
Night Ninja now!"
Gekko says.

"Super Gekko Muscles!"
Gekko says.

He takes the bus

from Night Ninja.

But Night Ninja steals

the Gekko-Mobile!

Gekko calls for help.

Owlette gets free.

Then she helps Catboy.

Together they help Gekko.

The PJ Masks toss
Night Ninja out of the
Gekko-Mobile.

"You will not beat me next time!"
Night Ninja says.

"When we help each other,
we cannot be beat!"
Gekko says.

The heroes return the bus to school!

Gekko learned that even
heroes need help sometimes.
Hooray for the PJ Masks!

PJMASKS
Owlette and the Giving Owl

Based on the episode
"Owlette and the Giving Owl"

Ready-to-Read

Simon Spotlight
New York   London   Toronto   Sydney   New Delhi

SIMON SPOTLIGHT
An imprint of Simon & Schuster Children's Publishing Division
1230 Avenue of the Americas, New York, New York 10020
This Simon Spotlight edition October 2018
Adapted by Daphne Pendergrass from the series PJ Masks
All rights reserved, including the right of reproduction in whole or in part in any form.
SIMON SPOTLIGHT, READY-TO-READ, and colophon are registered trademarks of
Simon & Schuster, Inc.
For information about special discounts for bulk purchases, please contact
Simon & Schuster Special Sales at 1-866-506-1949 or business@simonandschuster.com.
Manufactured in China 0718 SDI

Today is show-and-tell!
Amaya is excited to show the
class her giving owl statue.

"But your aunt told you to give away the statue," Connor says.

"Giving makes you feel good," Greg says. Amaya does not want to give away the statue.

Amaya, Greg, and Connor
walk into class.
Someone stole all the
show-and-tell things!

This looks like a job
for the PJ Masks!

Greg becomes Gekko!

Connor becomes

Catboy!

Amaya becomes Owlette!

They are the

PJ Masks!

Catboy hears
moths with his
Super Cat Ears.

The moths lead
them to Luna Girl!

Luna Girl goes to
steal more things.
The PJ Masks follow.

Oh no! Luna Girl steals the giving owl statue!

The statue is perfect. "I do not want the other stuff anymore," Luna Girl tells her moths.

"Let her keep the statue," Catboy tells Owlette. "She says she will return the other stuff."

"No!" Owlette says.

"It is mine!"

She takes the giving owl

from Luna Girl.

Luna Girl is mad.

She steals more stuff!

While the heroes put
the stolen things back,
Luna Girl takes
the giving owl again!
It is all she wants.

"Can she keep the statue?" Gekko asks. "You are supposed to give it away anyway."

Owlette does not want
to give away the
giving owl.

The PJ Masks return
to the Luna Lair.
There is a force field
around it.

Luna Girl jumps out!

She freezes Gekko

with her Luna Magnet!

Luna Girl freezes
Catboy too!

"Time to be a hero,"
Owlette says.
"You can have the
statue if you let Catboy
and Gekko go."

"No!" Luna Girl says.

She tries to freeze

Owlette next!

Owlette creates wind with her owl wings. The wind makes Luna Girl drop the statue and her Luna Magnet!

Gekko and Catboy are free!

Owlette takes the giving owl back.

"I am sorry," Luna Girl says.

Owlette feels bad for
Luna Girl. She gives her
the giving owl. Giving it
away does feel good!

The PJ Masks return
the show-and-tell things.
The day is saved!

PJMASKS
Race to the Moon!

Based on the episodes
"Moonstruck," parts 1 and 2

Ready-to-Read

Simon Spotlight
New York   London   Toronto   Sydney   New Delhi

SIMON SPOTLIGHT
An imprint of Simon & Schuster Children's Publishing Division
1230 Avenue of the Americas, New York, New York 10020
This Simon Spotlight edition October 2018
Adapted by Natalie Shaw from the series PJ Masks
All rights reserved, including the right of reproduction in whole or in part in any form.
SIMON SPOTLIGHT, READY-TO-READ, and colophon are registered trademarks of
Simon & Schuster, Inc.
For information about special discounts for bulk purchases, please contact
Simon & Schuster Special Sales at 1-866-506-1949 or business@simonandschuster.com.
Manufactured in China 0718 SDI

Amaya, Greg, and Connor
are learning about the moon.
When the moon looks orange
it is called a harvest moon.

It will happen tonight!
Luna Girl will be up to
no good.

This looks like a job
for the PJ Masks!

Greg becomes Gekko!

Connor becomes Catboy!

Amaya becomes Owlette!

They are the PJ Masks!

Now Luna Girl can travel
to the moon.
The harvest moon makes her
Luna Magnet stronger!

She wants to find the
harvest moon crystal.
It will make her so strong
that no one can stop her!

The PJ Masks have to go to the moon to stop Luna Girl.

PJ Robot can help.

He turns Headquarters
into a rocket ship!

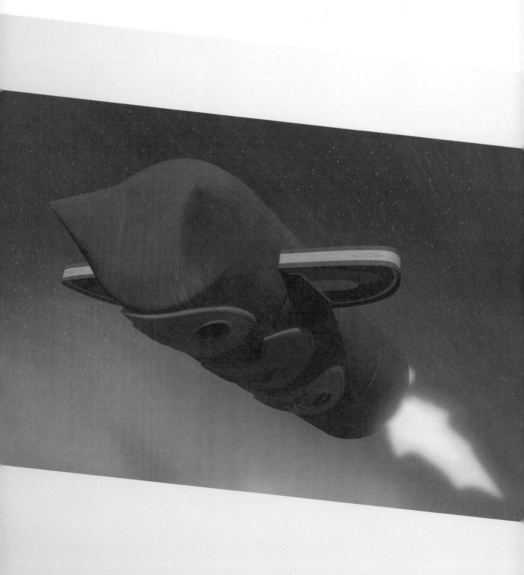

PJ Masks are on their way
into space to save the day!

Then Luna Girl throws
energy bubbles at their ship.

Owlette tries to keep

the ship safe.

It does not work!

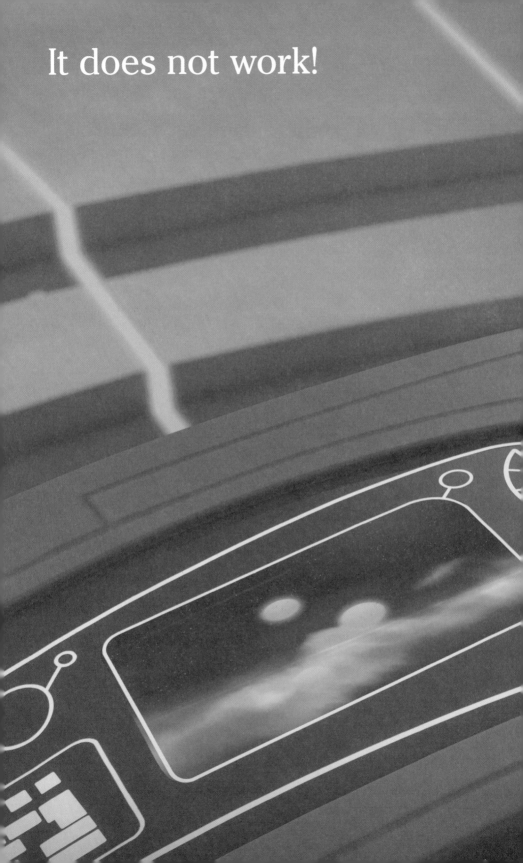

They have to land on
the moon.

Luna Girl is on the moon too!

The PJ Masks race out
on their PJ Rovers.

They are too late.

Luna Girl finds the

harvest moon crystal!

The PJ Masks have to
stop her!
Catboy tries to use
his Super Cat Speed.

It does not work!

Luna Girl laughs.

Their powers
do not work the same
on the moon.

Luna Girl uses the crystal
to make a trap
around the PJ Masks.

They escape

when Gekko uses his

Super Gekko Muscles!

The heroes break free
from the trap!

They work together to get the harvest moon crystal.

The PJ Masks saved

the moon!

PJ Masks Save the Library!

Based on the episode
"Owlette and the Flash Flip Trip"

Ready-to-Read

Simon Spotlight
New York   London   Toronto   Sydney   New Delhi

SIMON SPOTLIGHT
An imprint of Simon & Schuster Children's Publishing Division
1230 Avenue of the Americas, New York, New York 10020
This Simon Spotlight edition October 2018
Adapted by Daphne Pendergrass from the series PJ Masks
All rights reserved, including the right of reproduction in whole or in part in any form.
SIMON SPOTLIGHT, READY-TO-READ, and colophon are registered trademarks of
Simon & Schuster, Inc.
For information about special discounts for bulk purchases, please contact
Simon & Schuster Special Sales at 1-866-506-1949 or business@simonandschuster.com.
Manufactured in China 0718 SDI

Amaya is excited to read her Flossy Flash superhero book.

Oh no! Someone erased
all the stories!
The books just have
pictures of Romeo inside!

This looks like a job
for the PJ Masks!

Greg becomes Gekko!

Connor becomes Catboy!

Amaya becomes Owlette!

They are the

PJ Masks!

Owlette is reading
her Flossy Flash book.

She wants to be
like Flossy Flash.

In the Cat-Car,
Catboy asks Owlette
to use her Owl Eyes
to find Romeo.

Owlette wants powers
like Flossy Flash instead.

Catboy hears Romeo
with his Super Cat Ears.

Oh no! Romeo ruined more books and is escaping!

"Where will Romeo
go next?" Catboy asks.

"To the library!"

Gekko shouts.

"We have to stop him!"

The heroes make a plan.
Gekko climbs high with
his Super Lizard Grip.

He asks Owlette to look
for Romeo with her
Owl Eyes.

Instead, she pretends to be Flossy Flash!

She forgets to look

for Romeo!

"Robot!" Owlette cries
when she sees Romeo and
his robot.

Owlette is too late.

Romeo ties up

Gekko and Catboy!

"I will save you with
my Flossy Flash Flip!"
Owlette says.

Owlette trips and falls.

Romeo laughs and steals

all the library books!

"I should have used
my owl powers,"
Owlette says.

"Time to be a hero!"
she says. She sets
Catboy and Gekko free.

She uses her Owl Eyes
and Super Owl Wings
to look for Romeo.

She sees Romeo.

"I still have my book!"

she shouts.

Romeo and his robot
chase her!
Catboy and Gekko
tie up the robot!

The PJ Masks fix all

the books.

They save the library!

Super Cat Speed!

Based on the screenplay
"Catboy's Great Gig"

Ready-to-Read

Simon Spotlight
New York   London   Toronto   Sydney   New Delhi

SIMON SPOTLIGHT
An imprint of Simon & Schuster Children's Publishing Division
1230 Avenue of the Americas, New York, New York 10020
This Simon Spotlight edition October 2018
Adapted by Cala Spinner from the series PJ Masks
All rights reserved, including the right of reproduction in whole or in part in any form.
SIMON SPOTLIGHT, READY-TO-READ, and colophon are registered trademarks of
Simon & Schuster, Inc.
For information about special discounts for bulk purchases, please contact
Simon & Schuster Special Sales at 1-866-506-1949 or business@simonandschuster.com.
Manufactured in China 0718 SDI

The school concert
is tomorrow.

But where are

the instruments?

This is a job
for the PJ Masks!

Amaya becomes Owlette!

Greg becomes Gekko!

Connor becomes Catboy!

They are the PJ Masks!

Catboy is scared.

He does not want

to play in the concert.

What if he messes up?

The PJ Masks hear

a harsh noise.

It is Night Ninja!

Night Ninja is singing.

The Ninjalinos have
the missing instruments.

Catboy will use his
Super Cat Leap
to trap the Ninjalinos
with a net.

But he is too afraid.

It does not work.

"If we cannot get the instruments back, I guess the concert is off," says Owlette.

Catboy does not like
to see his friend sad.

Catboy uses Super Cat Speed!

He speeds around

the Ninjalinos.

He takes back one of
the instruments.
It is a recorder.

Catboy will need to play the recorder. Everyone is watching, but Catboy must be brave.

Catboy plays the recorder.

He is really good!

The Ninjalinos like
playing with Catboy
more than Night Ninja.

They leave Night Ninja!

Then Owlette and Gekko
trap Night Ninja in a drum.

The Ninjalinos give
the instruments back.
"I will get you for this!"
Night Ninja says.

PJ Masks all shout hooray!

Because in the night,

we saved the day!

Catboy learned that
it is okay to be afraid,
but always do your best!